Lottie Loves Music!

Written by Tom Ottway

Illustrated by Eya Mordyakova

Collins

What's in this story?

Listen and say

queen

violin

harp

piano

alien

drum

flute

Lottie's at her music lesson.
The teacher says, "Watch me, Lottie!
I'm playing the violin."

The teacher says, "Now you try, Lottie!"

One, two, three ...

But Lottie isn't listening! She's playing
with an orchestra!

The teacher says, "Stop, Lottie! Stop!"

The teacher is playing the flute.
He says, "Try the flute, Lottie!"

But Lottie isn't listening! She's playing to the animals!

The teacher says, "Stop, Lottie! Stop!"

The teacher is playing the harp.

But Lottie isn't listening! She's playing to the fish.

The teacher says, "Stop, Lottie! Stop!"

Lottie is playing the piano.
The teacher says, "Stop Lottie! Copy me!"

But Lottie isn't listening! She's playing to the aliens.

The teacher says, "Stop, Lottie! Stop!"

The teacher is playing the drum.

But Lottie isn't listening! She's playing to the Queen!

The teacher says, "Stop, Lottie! Stop!"

The teacher says, "Let's sing, Lottie.
You and me!"

Yes, Lottie is listening now!

Yes, Lottie is listening!
Lottie is learning!

19

Lottie's singing at the school!
She's singing with the orchestra.

Picture dictionary

Listen and repeat

alien

drum

flute

harp

orchestra

piano

queen

violin

1 Look and order the story

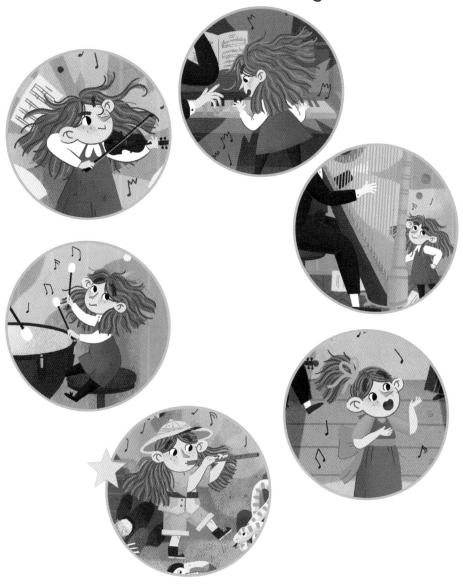

2 Listen and say

Collins

Published by Collins
An imprint of HarperCollins*Publishers*
Westerhill Road
Bishopbriggs
Glasgow
G64 2QT

HarperCollins*Publishers*
1st Floor, Watermarque Building
Ringsend Road
Dublin 4
Ireland

William Collins' dream of knowledge for all began with the publication of his first book in 1819.

A self-educated mill worker, he not only enriched millions of lives, but also founded a flourishing publishing house. Today, staying true to this spirit, Collins books are packed with inspiration, innovation and practical expertise. They place you at the centre of a world of possibility and give you exactly what you need to explore it.

© HarperCollins*Publishers* Limited 2020

10 9 8 7 6 5 4 3 2 1

ISBN 978-0-00-839777-7

Collins® and COBUILD® are registered trademarks of HarperCollins*Publishers* Limited

www.collins.co.uk/elt

Author: Tom Ottway
Illustrator: Eya Mordyakova (Beehive)
Series editor: Rebecca Adlard
Publishing manager: Lisa Todd
Product managers: Jennifer Hall and Caroline Green
In-house editor: Alma Puts Keren
Project manager: Emily Hooton
Editor: Deborah Friedland
Proofreaders: Natalie Murray and Michael Lamb
Cover designer: Kevin Robbins
Typesetter: 2Hoots Publishing Services Ltd
Audio produced by id audio, London
Reading guide author: Emma Wilkinson
Production controller: Rachel Weaver
Printed and bound by: GPS Group, Slovenia

MIX
Paper from
responsible sources

FSC
www.fsc.org

FSC™ C007454

This book is produced from independently certified FSC™ paper to ensure responsible forest management.

For more information visit: **www.harpercollins.co.uk/green**

Download the audio for this book and a reading guide for parents and teachers at www.collins.co.uk/839777